东汉张芝圣跡图
大唐玄奘圣迹图

DRAWINGS OF ZHANG ZHI SAINT DEEDS
IN THE EASTERN HAN DYNASTY
DRAWINGS OF XUANZANG SAINT DEEDS
IN THE TANG DYNASTY

董振中　绘

敦煌文艺出版社

图书在版编目（C I P）数据

东汉张芝圣迹图·大唐玄奘圣迹图 / 董振中绘 . --
兰州：敦煌文艺出版社，2017.12
　ISBN 978-7-5468-1391-2

　I . ①东… II . ①董… III . ①中国画—人物画—作品
集—中国—现代 IV . ① J222.7

　中国版本图书馆 CIP 数据核字 (2017) 第 277461 号

东汉张芝圣迹图·大唐玄奘圣迹图
董振中　绘

出　版　人：王永生
责任编辑：杨继军　赵润瑜
装帧设计：马吉庆

敦煌文艺出版社出版、发行
地址：（730030）兰州市城关区读者大道 568 号
邮箱：dunhuangwenyi1958@163.com
0931-8773114（编辑部）
0931-8773112　8773235（发行部）

雅昌文化（集团）有限公司印刷
开本 889 毫米 ×1194 毫米　1/12　印张 10　插页 5　字数 25 千
2018 年 3 月第 1 版　2018 年 3 月第 1 次印刷
印数：1 ~ 5000

ISBN 978-7-5468-1391-2
定价：388.00 元

策　划

瓜州县人民政府

中共瓜州县委宣传部

瓜州县文化体育局

编　辑

瓜州县文物局

瓜州县草圣文化传媒有限责任公司

瓜州县草圣张芝书画有限责任公司

董振中，字子午，号老草，1945 年生，山东人。1968 年毕业于浙江美术学院（现中国美术学院），中国美术家协会会员，国家一级美术师，中央电视台特聘画师，北京中国画研究院画师。曾任山东省邹城市美术家协会主席、邹城市画院院长，现定居深圳。我国当今画坛卓有成就并享有盛誉的艺术家。已出版的作品有《董振中画集》《董振中国画小品集》《国画人物名家董振中》《至圣孔子》《亚圣孟子》《孔子圣迹图》《孟子圣迹图》《孔门圣贤图》《水浒英雄谱》等。曾在济南、深圳、广州、杭州、香港、澳门等地举办画展，并先后赴意大利、日本、加拿大、印度尼西亚、阿联酋、俄罗斯、马来西亚、法国、荷兰等十几个国家举办个人作品展览。

Dong Zhenzhong, alias Ziwu, another name Laocao, was born in 1945. He is from the hometown of Confucius. He graduated from China Academy of Art. He is a member of China Artists Association, first-class artist of the nation, specially recruited painter of CCTV and the painter of Beijing Chinese Painting Research Institute. He used to be the president of Shandong Zoucheng Artists Association and the president of Zoucheng Painting Institute. Now he lives in Shenzhen. He is a successful painter in our country's painting circle and enjoys a great reputation. He published *Dong Zhenzhong Paintings, Dong Zhenzhong Short and Simple Traditional Chinese Painting Collection, A Famous Figure of Traditional Chinese Painting Dong Zhenzhong, Confucius, Mencius, Confucius's Relics, Mencius Relics, Pictures of Confucian Saints and Wise Men, A Book of Shuihu Heroes,* etc. He used to host painting exhibitions in Jinan, Shenzhen, Guangzhou, Hangzhou, Hong Kong, Macao, etc., and had been to Italy, Japan, Canada, Indonesia, United Arab Emirates, Russia, Malaysia, France, Holland, etc. to host personal work exhibition.

大唐玄奘圣迹图
Drawings of Xuanzang saint deeds in the Tang Dynasty

东漢張芝聖跡圖

董振中

DRAWINGS OF
ZHANG ZHI
SAINT DEEDS IN
THE EASTERN
HAN DYNASTY

东汉张芝

张 芝

Zhang Zhi

东汉时期，有着"书中四贤"之称的张芝出生在华夏文明的重要发祥地——甘肃瓜州（古渊泉）。

张芝，字伯英，出身名门。从小就无心政治，一门心思钻研书法。张芝擅长草书中的章草，将当时字字区别、笔画分离的草法，改为上下牵连富于变化的新写法，富有独创性，影响很大，有"草圣"之称。书迹今无墨迹传世，仅北宋《淳化阁帖》中收有他的《八月帖》等刻帖。

张芝刻苦练习书法的精神，历史上已传为佳话。晋卫恒《四体书势》中记载：张芝"凡家中衣帛，必书而后练（煮染）之；临池学书，池水尽墨"。后人称书法为"临池"，即来源于此。当时的人珍爱其墨甚至到了"寸纸不遗"的地步。对张芝的评价相当高，尤以草书为最。

一笔飞贯，开书法艺术汪洋恣肆之先河；千年独步，树古今书坛屹立不朽之丰碑。草圣张芝不仅为书法界屹立了丰碑，也为后人留下了宝贵的精神财富。

During the Eastern Han Dynasty, Zhang Zhi, with the title of "Four Talents of Calligraphy", was born in Gaunsu Guazhou (the ancient Yuanquan County)—an important cradle of Huaxia culture.

Zhang Zhi, another name Boying, was of noble origin. He had no interest in politics when he was young and was dedicated to calligraphy. Zhang Zhi was good at zhangcao (a specific kind of cursive hand of Chinese calligraphy). He changed the traditional cursive hand in which characters and strokes were separate into a new type of writing in which the characters and strokes were connected. This is of originality and great influence. He has the title of cursive hand prodigy. None of his works is passed to this day. Only his *August Handwriting Book* was included in the Song Dynasty's *Chunhua Pavilion Handwriting Book*.

Zhang Zhi's assiduity in practicing calligraphy had become a much-told story in history. Wei Heng's *Si Ti Shu Shi* (the earliest and reliable book on calligraphy theory) of Jin Dynasty recorded that: "all clothes and silk at Zhang Zhi's house were written characters by Zhang Zhi, then they were washed; when Zhang Zhi learned calligraphy beside the pool, the water in the pool all become black". That's why later generations call calligraphy "linchi" (pinyin for beside the pool). The people of Zhang Zhi's time liked his calligraphy very much; they even didn't leave a cun of his writing out". The evaluation of his writing is rather high, especially his cursive script; it's the most praised.

Using a flying writing brush to create the start of the bold, unconstrained and free calligraphy art; a unique style for a thousand of years established an immortal monument in ancient and modern calligraphers' circles. The cursive script prodigy Zhang Zhi not only erected a monument for calligraphers' circles, but also had left great spiritual treasure for later generations.

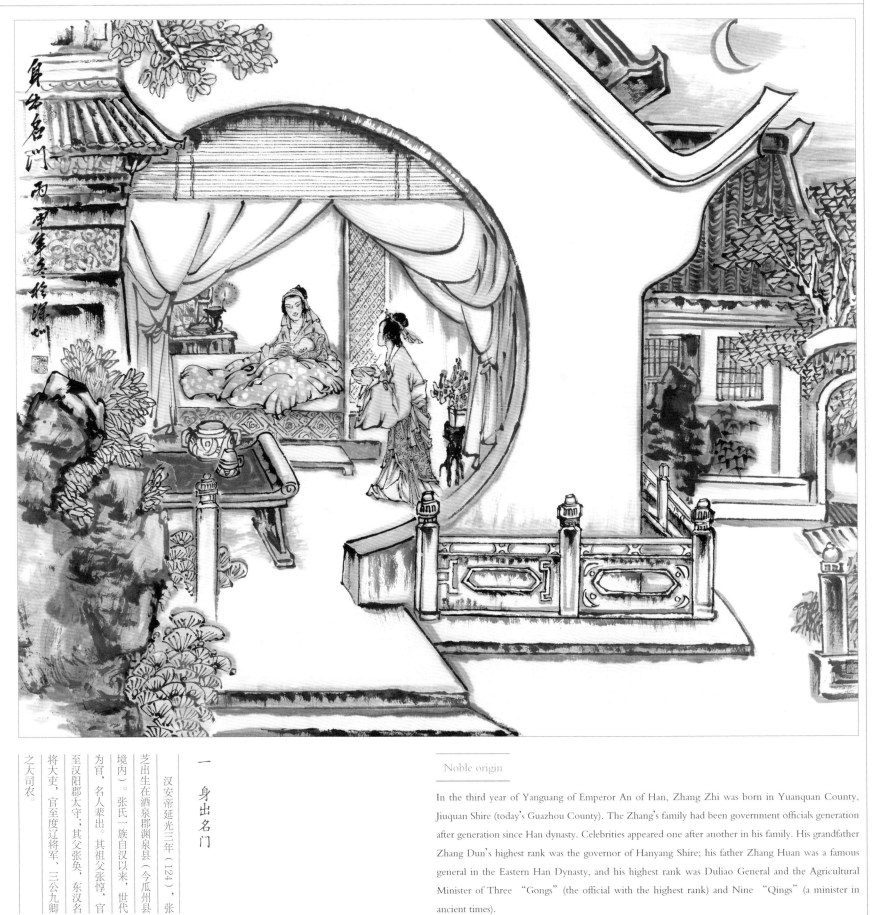

一 身出名门

汉安帝延光三年（124），张芝出生在酒泉郡渊泉县（今瓜州县境内）。张氏一族自汉以来，世代为官，名人辈出。其祖父张惇，官至汉阳郡太守；其父张奂，东汉名将大吏，官至度辽将军、三公九卿之大司农。

Noble origin

In the third year of Yanguang of Emperor An of Han, Zhang Zhi was born in Yuanquan County, Jiuquan Shire (today's Guazhou County). The Zhang's family had been government officials generation after generation since Han dynasty. Celebrities appeared one after another in his family. His grandfather Zhang Dun's highest rank was the governor of Hanyang Shire; his father Zhang Huan was a famous general in the Eastern Han Dynasty, and his highest rank was Duliao General and the Agricultural Minister of Three "Gongs" (the official with the highest rank) and Nine "Qings" (a minister in ancient times).

Given the name of
Zhang Zhi

When his mother Mrs. Wei was giving birth to her first daughter, she used
to dream that a huge lucid ganoderma (in Chinese phonetic alphabet lucid
ganoderma is "lingzhi") was growing in the garden, so her daughter was
given the name Zhang Ling; in order to form the meaning of lingzhi(lucid
ganoderma), his grandfather Zhang Dun named him Zhang Zhi, with the
style name of Boying.

二 取名张芝

母亲尉氏在生女儿时，曾梦见
花园内生长出一株硕大的灵芝，因
而为女儿取名张灵。爷爷张惇亦取
灵芝之意，为孙儿取名张芝，字伯
英。

三 周岁抓笔

孩子长大必是个读书之人。

空中比画，视而不顾，伸手直取毛笔，

百物，大家一阵欢呼，认为

铜钱摆了一席。小张芝面对琳琅

周、玩具、糕点、文房四宝、金银、

习俗，张府宴请亲友，看孩子抓

在张芝周岁生日这天，依据

Grabbed a writing brush when
he was one year old

When Zhang Zhi was having his 1st birthday, the Zhang's family held a banquet and invited their family
members and friends to look at the child "zhuazhou" (a ceremony held when the new-born baby is
one year old. During the ceremony, parents put all sorts of objects before the baby to let him choose one.)
In the face of the many beautiful things, little Zhang Zhi ignored them, chose a writing brush directly,
and gesticulated in the air. Everyone was excited and cheering; they thought that the baby must be a
scholar when he grew up.

Hire a teacher to enlighten Zhang Zhi

When Zhang Zhi was a child, he loved reading poetry, singing prose and verses and writing. Zhang Huan was very delighted. He hired a famous local teacher and earnestly entrusted him to teach his son to read and write. Being a talented boy, Zhang Zhi was greatly praised by his teacher.

四 延师启蒙

张芝孩提之时，即喜爱吟诗唱赋，握笔习字。张奂甚喜，特延请当地名师，殷殷嘱托，教授几子读书习字，进行启蒙教育。张芝天资聪颖，深得老师嘉许。

五　送父进京

老太守张惇在孙子五岁那年去世。张芝八岁时，张奂守丧满三年，决意去京城洛阳博取功名。在离开家乡之际，他跟八岁的儿子告别。小张芝却道："父亲尽管放心前去，家中自有我来。"父母亲听了，又好笑，又欣慰。

Send his father to Luoyang

The old governor Zhang Dun died when his grandson was five years old. When Zhang Zhi was eight years old, the period of Zhang Huan's keeping vigil beside the coffin had reached three years, and he decided to go to the capital Luoyang to win high official positions. While he was leaving his hometown, he said goodbye to his eight-year-old son. But little Zhang Zhi said, "Father, go with ease. I will take care of the family." After his parents heard this, they felt funny and gratified.

Play truant and meet with a mishap

After his father left home, another side of little Zhang Zhi began to reveal: a naughty boy who became very fond of play. Once, taking advantage of the opportunity that his teacher was absent, he took his younger brother Zhang Chang away from the classroom and played in the forest. However, to their surprise, they walked into the recesses of the forest. Because his younger brother picked flowers everywhere, he was poisoned by an anonymous toxicant, and became red and swollen all over.

六　逃学遇险

父亲离家后，小张芝露出了孩童贪玩的天性。一次趁先生不在，竟带着弟弟张昶离开学堂，到树林去玩耍，不想一直走到林子深处。因弟弟到处采花，不知中了什么毒，浑身红肿。

七　断炊教子

母亲知道后，非常生气，便把兄弟二人叫到面前，立刻把炉膛里正旺的柴火抽出灭掉，兄弟俩惊愕不解。母亲指着锅里的米饭说："现在这锅里的米饭就成了夹生饭，即使再生火加热，也不会熟，更不会好吃。读书学习如果中断，也就像这夹生饭。"小张芝立刻明白了母亲的良苦用心。

Stop cooking to teach her sons

After his mother knew, she was very angry. So she brought the two brothers before her, and quenched the fire in the stove. The two brothers were very surprised and confused. Their mother pointed at the rice in the cook pot and said, "Now the rice in the cook pot becomes half-cooked. Even if you light a fire and cook it again, it will not be done, let alone delicious. If you suspend your study, it will be like this half-cooked rice." Little Zhang Zhi immediately understood his mother's care and thought.

The two brothers
progress together

From then on Zhang Zhi regretted very much.
He realized his mistakes even more, and became
hardworking and self-disciplined. He studied
diligently and was no longer lazy. When the two
brothers practiced calligraphy, they were especially
focused, and made great progress in study.

八　兄弟齐驱

自此张芝后悔不已，便更加
警醒，勤奋自律，勤学不惰；兄
弟二人练字尤为专注，学业大进，
先生不断称赞，认为二人将来不
是文宗亦是将表。

柳不惜书
丁酉年之夏月
宁玉深圳

九　柳下学书

张家门口，绿树环抱，浓荫蔽
日，清静优美，一湾池水清澈透明。
池边柳树下，有石板雕成的桌凳，
张芝和弟弟在此读书练字。

Learning under the willow

In front of Zhang's door, there were many willows. The shadow warded off the sun. This was a quiet and beautiful place. And there was a pool with clear and transparent water. Under the willow next to the pool several stone desks and chairs were carved, so that Zhang Zhi and his brother could read books and practice calligraphy here.

Learning Cui &Du for
the first time

When the Han Dynasty became prosperous, cursive script appeared. At the time of Emperor Zhang of Han Dynasty, there was a person good at writing, his name is Du Du. His writing and drawing were slightly thin, large and robust. Later there were Cui Yuan and Cui Shi. Their writing style was dense, and the structure was delicate and ingenious. Under the promotion of Cui Yuan, Cui Shi and Du Du, cursive script had become an independent writing style. Zhang Zhi liked it very much and learned it. He gathered their essence, absorbed their advantages and learned their excellence.

十　初学崔杜

汉兴而有草书，至章帝时，齐相杜度，号称善作，字画微瘦，杰有骨力。后有崔瑗、崔实，书体甚浓，结字工巧。在崔杜推动之下，草书已成独立书体。张芝喜而学之，采精收华，遍纳崔杜之长，学尽崔杜之妙。

十一　池水尽墨

张芝兄弟池边习字不倦，以笔蘸水，以水研墨，以水洗砚，久而久之池水逐渐变黑，被人称为墨池。晋卫恒《四体书势》曰：『临池学书，池水尽墨。』后人称书法为『临池』，即来源于此。张芝善书善思，好学百家，弟弟张昶（被后人称为亚圣），亦有书法天赋，尤善章草。

The pool water was full of ink

The Zhang Zhi brothers were incessant in their practicing of calligraphy by the pool. They used the writing brush to dip in the water, used the water to grind the ink and used the water to wash the inkstone. After a long time, the water in the pool gradually became black, and the pool was named ink pool since. Wei Heng in Jin Dynasty wrote in his book Si Ti Shu Shi (the earliest and a reliable book on calligraphy theory) that, "when learning calligraphy by the pool, the pool water all became black." Afterwards people in later generations call calligraphy "Linchi" (Linchi, the Chinese phonetic alphabet for "by the pool"). Zhang Zhi was good at writing and thinking, and enjoyed learning different academic schools. His brother Zhang Chang was also gifted in calligraphy. He was especially good at "zhangcao" (a specific kind of cursive hand of Chinese calligraphy). He was named "yasheng" (a title given to a person when his/her academic achievements are extremely high but is secondary to another) by later generations.

Sending his sister to get married

During the first years of Yongchu, the Eastern Han Dynasty, the Qiang people invaded Anding Shire. After receiving the imperial edict, Zhang Huan, as the military officer, led troops to the border to fight the qiang people. At this time, the daughter Zhang Ling had been engaged with Suo's family from Dunhuang, and she had come to the age of marriage. Since Zhang Huan couldn't desert his post and delay the combat opportunity, Zhang Ling's marriage had to be handled by Zhang Zhi, in representation of his father. Since it was war time and the situation was hasty, Zhang Ling could only make the marriage ceremony simple and omit many links according to his father's arrangement.

十二 送姊出閣

东汉永初年间，羌人攻入安定郡内，张奂奉旨以中郎衔带兵赴边。这时女儿张灵已和敦煌索家订婚，并已到了婚嫁年龄。由于张奂不能擅离职守，贻误战机，张灵的婚礼只好由儿子张芝之代办。由于正值战乱时期，时间仓促，婚礼一切从简，省去了许多环节。张芝只好按父亲的安排，婚礼一切从简，省去了许多环节。

十三　敦煌求学

初逾黄口，张芝即以少有大志、敏而好学而闻名乡里。舞勺之年，遵从父亲安排，前往敦煌求学，全面学习经史子集。数年间，其学业素养和书法功力得到很大提升。

Study at Dunhuang

When Zhang Zhi had just grown up from a child, he had become famous in his hometown. When he was 13 years old, he went to Dunhuang to study according to his father's arrangement, learning Confucian Classics, novels, history, geography, The Hundred Schools of Thought, poetry, ci(a type of classical Chinese poetry), fu(descriptive prose interspersed with verse), etc. After many years, his academic quality and calligraphy skill improved greatly.

Making a lot of genuine
friends

During his many years of study in Dunhuang, Zhang Zhi made friends with books. He met the adultlike, magnanimous and studious Suo Jingsha who had a gift in calligraphy; he met the handsome Huangpu Song who could not only perform martial art but also was educated; he met honest and studious Qiu Jing who could do first-class calligraphy. They formed a group with literature and learned from each other by exchanging views, benefiting enormously.

十四 广交挚友

敦煌求学数年，张芝以书会友，结识了老成大度、好学善书的索静沙、倜傥英俊、文武兼备的皇甫嵩、耿直好学、书法一流的仇靖等一帮挚友。大家以文结社，经常切磋，得益匪浅。

十五　杂糅百家

张芝行走于市井乡里，拜访民间书艺高手大家，共同探讨各种书体之优劣，求教交流，如饥似渴。揣摩各种字体独特之处，汲取各种艺术精粹，海纳百川，杂糅百家，全面提升书艺内涵。

Mix a hundred
schools of thoughts

Zhang Zhi walks among towns and villages and visited folk talents and masters of calligraphy. He discussed the advantages and disadvantages of various types of writing styles. He asked for advice from the masters and communicated with them on calligraphy. He was thirsting and hungering for knowledge. He also carefully studied the uniqueness of all types of fonts, absorbed the artistic essence of various types of writing. He absorbed a lot of different types of writing style and mixed a hundred schools of thoughts, improving his calligraphy connotation comprehensively.

Learn martial art under
the moon

At that time it was the Mid−autumn, the bright moon hung above the sky. A group of
teenagers—Zhang Zhi, Zhang Chang, Huangpu Song, etc., exercised and learned martial art.
Zhang Zhi held a sword in his hand, made a movement with a rush. His two eyes were like
meteors, brandishing with high spirit. The sword was brandished faster, like a silver dragon, turning
up and down, coiling left and right. He brandished like a flying dragon, and brandished as fast as a
thunder light. There was wind where his sword passed. His skills reached the acme of perfection.

十六　月下习武

时值中秋、明月高悬，张芝、张昶、皇甫嵩等一帮年轻人，健身习武。只见张芝握剑在手，刷地亮开架势，两只眼睛像流星般一闪，精神抖擞地舞了起来。那剑越舞越快，就像一条银龙上下翻飞，左右盘绕，动若飞龙，疾若闪电，宝剑过处，习习生风，出神入化。

十七　进京寻父

转眼张奂进京已十多年了，脚跟站稳，又有了皇恩庇护，才想到把儿子召进京来，子从父参军打仗，当时已成惯例。张芝收到父亲来信，立刻收拾行囊，告别母亲，进京寻父。

Went to the capital
to look for his father

In a short time, it had been more than ten years since Zhang Huan went to the capital. He had established his career there, and had been protected by imperial favour. So he wanted to call his son into the capital. It had been a custom for sons to follow their fathers in the army. When Zhang Zhi received his father's letter, he immediately packed his luggage, said farewell to his mother, and went to the capital to look for his father.

Sell calligraphy to save his father

Although Zhang Huan made many contributions during war, since Liangji Event was reported, he had been framed up by eunuchs and dominating ministers. He was chained and thrown into prison. Zhang Zhi came to the capital Luoyang, he found no kin to turn to, his travelling expenses were running out, he was isolated and helpless. When he asked for help everywhere, he couldn't find anyone to help him. So he could only set a table in the street and sell his calligraphy while inquiring about his father's old friends to save his father.

十八 卖字救父

张奂虽屡立战功，由于梁冀事发，受到牵连，遭到宦官、权臣的陷害，锒铛入狱。张芝来到京城洛阳，举目无亲，盘缠用尽，孤立无援，四处求告无门，只好立案当街，一边写字卖字，一边打听父亲的旧时好友，想办法搭救父亲。

十九　誉满京城

张芝身高八尺，英俊潇洒，一表人才。书法气势磅礴，如同横空出世，名震京师。一时购者如云，京城的人们都认识了这位当街卖字的年轻人。

Zhang Zhi was eight feet tall, and was handsome and good-looking. His calligraphy was grand and magnificent. He soared across the sky and made a great reputation in the city. People all went to buy his calligraphy. All people in capital became aware of this young man who sold calligraphy in street.

Visit Huangpu Gui

Although Zhang Huan had a lot of old friends, they were all afraid
that they would be implicated by him, so none of them took Zhang
Zhi in. Only Duliao General Huangpu Gui took him in, and wrote
a visiting name card immediately, and asked Zhang Zhi to pay a
formal visit to East Sea Prime Minister Huang Fu, begging him to
write a memorial to the throne to tell the truth, to ask the emperor
to forgive Zhang Huan and remit his punishment.

二十　拜见皇甫规

张奂旧友虽多，可由于害怕牵
连，无人敢接纳张芝，只有度辽
将军皇甫规纳其入内，并当即写
了拜帖，让张芝去拜见东海相黄
浮，求其向皇上上表，为张奂辩白，
求皇上开恩教免。

二十一 一进黄府

张芝带着拜帖，进了黄府。拜
见黄浮后，张芝向他诉说父亲张
奂的冤屈。东海相黄浮乃正直敢
为之士，已知道张奂是被人陷害，
当即答应张芝，上表皇上，为其
父辩白。

Enter Huang's mansion
for the first time

Zhang Zhi took the visiting name card and entered Huang's mansion.
After visiting Huang Fu, Zhang Zhi told him his father's grievances.
East Sea Prime Minister Huang Fu was a very honest and brave
person. He had already known that Zhang Huan was framed up, so he
promised Zhang Zhi that he would write a memorial to the throne to
tell Zhang Huan's innocence.

初識黃芙蓉

翠云軒月

東漢張芝聖跡圖

Met Huang Furong
for the first time

When they were talking in the back yard, suddenly, a young general in red clothes burst in the yard, riding. When the general just arrived in front of them, Zhang Zhi recognized that the young general in red clothes was the handsome childe who bought his calligraphy the day before yesterday. The general also recognized that the person in front of her was the youth who sold calligraphy in the street. The two smiled at each other unanimously. Huang Fu pointed at the young general in red clothes and said, "this is my daughter Huang Furong. Since I have no son, I educate her like a son."

二十二 初識黃芙蓉

两人正在后院说话，突然有一红衣小将骑马闯进院来。刚一到面前，张芝就认出红衣小将正是前天买字的俊公子，来者也认出面前之人正是当街卖字的青年。两人不约而同地相视一笑。黄浮却指着红衣小将说："这是小女芙蓉，因膝下无子，就将其当几子一样调教。"

二鈺黄府
丁酉年之秋日恒深竹達姬中

二十三　二进黄府

在皇甫规、黄浮等人的解救
下，张奂被无罪释放。张奂带着
儿子张芝到黄府拜谢。张奂见到
黄浮，感谢搭救之恩。黄芙蓉见
到张芝非常欢喜，二人各有爱意。
张奂看在眼里，便试着代儿子向
黄浮求亲，那黄浮也多次听女儿
夸奖张芝，当即便答应了这门亲
事。

Enter Huang's mansion
for the second time

With the help of Huangpu Gui and Huang Fu, Zhang Huan was acquitted of the charge.
Zhang Huan took his son to Huang's mansion to thank him. When Zhang Huan saw
Huang Fu, he thanked him for his help. When Huang Furong saw Zhang Zhi, she was
very happy. The two had good feelings for each other. Zhang Huan was aware of this,
so he tried to seek a marriage alliance to Huang Fu for his son. Huang Fu also heard his
daughter praising Zhang Zhi often, so he agreed to the marriage immediately.

A grand wedding ceremony
in Zhang's mansion

The new Zhang's mansion built in Luoyang was decorated with lanterns and colored hangings, and was full of the sound of drum and music. And all friends and family members attended the wedding. According to his father's intention, the oldest son in Zhang's mansion married Huang Furong—the daughter of East Sea Prime Minister Huang Fu. The wedding was hosted by Zhang Huan's good friend Suo Yi. After the two had Xitao ceremony, Duixi ceremony, Tonglao ceremony, Hejin ceremony, Jieying ceremony and Jiefa ceremony, the young couple was sent to the bridal chamber.

二十四 张府大婚

洛阳新盖的张府内，张灯结彩，鼓乐齐鸣，高朋满座。张府长子伯英受父命大婚，聘东海相黄浮之女黄芙蓉为妻。婚礼由张奂好友索一主持。在双方举行沈绦礼、对席礼、同牢礼、合卺礼、解缨礼、结发礼后送入洞房。

二十五 春游白马寺

美观挺拔，真乃世间难得珍品。

刻凤，极尽工巧，笔尖色泽光润，

侈之极，笔管上描金绘银，雕龙

再看那笔墨纸砚，就那笔已是奢

四宝一套吧。"张芝忙叩头谢恩。

你书法名满京城，朕就赐你文房

父边关作战立功不少，朕也听说

过张芝卖字救父的事，便道："你

将军的长子张芝。桓帝也早听说

侍臣忙对桓帝禀告："这便是张奂

刘志也来白马寺上香，君臣偶遇，

妇至白马寺祈福许愿。此时桓帝

春暖花开，张芝、黄芙蓉夫

A tour in Baima Temple

In warm spring, flowers are coming out with a rush. Zhang Zhi and Huang Furong went to Baima Temple to pray for happiness and wish for success. At this time Emperor Huan Liu Zhi also came to Baima Temple to pray. When the emperor and the Zhang Zhi met accidently, the near official reported to Emperor Huan that this was General Zhang Huan's oldest son Zhang Zhi. Emperor Huan also heard the story that Zhang Zhi sold his calligraphy to save his father, so he said, "Your father had made a lot of contributions during the war in the border. I also heard that your calligraphy made you famous in the capital. I will grant you four precious articles of the writing table." Zhang Zhi immediately kowtowed and thanked the emperor for his favor. The pen sent by the emperor was extremely luxurious. Gold and silver lines were drawn on the pen. A dragon and phoenix were also carved on the pen. The pen was extremely fine and delicate. The pen point's color and luster were smooth & glossy and beautiful & forceful. It was indeed a rare treasure in the world.

随父亲征 空言辅征圣迹图

Go out to battle with his
father

In 163 A.D., the war in the northwest border was incessant.
Emperor Huan gave an imperial order that appointed
Zhonglang General(military officer) Zhang Huan as Duliao
General and ordered him to go out to battle. According to
custom, Zhang Zhi also wore military uniform, rode a military
horse and went to the border war field with his father.

二十六　随父出征

公元一六三年，西北边疆战火
不断，桓帝下旨，升中郎将张奂为
度辽将军，带兵出征。按惯例张芝
也身着戎装，骑着战马，随父亲来
到边疆战场。

二十七 沙场立功

张芝随父亲来到西北军营，见战旗猎猎，士兵斗志昂扬。张芝弓马娴熟，有胆有识，屡战屡胜。随父出征几年中，张家父子多次击败羌人、匈奴，平息了边疆叛乱，为汉立下大功。

Make a contribution
in the war

Zhang Zhi followed his father and come to northwest military camp. There he saw the floating war flag and high-spirited soldiers. Zhang Zhi was proficient with bow and horse, and had courage and insight. They had won every battle. During the years when he was serving in the army, Zhang Zhi and his father defeated the invasion of Qiang people and the Hun(an ancient nationality in China), and suppressed the revolt in the border, making a great contribution to Han Dynasty.

二十八　无意仕途

东汉末年，外戚和宦官轮番掌
权，社会动荡不堪。许多仁人志
士如李膺、陈蕃、王畅等不畏强暴，
奋起反抗，但或被处死、或被流放，
或被禁锢。自此以后，士人忘口，
万马齐喑，整个国家陷入动荡和
混乱之中。加上父亲多次遭到权
臣、宦官的陷害，让张芝无意仕途，
谢绝了皇上的一切赏赐，专注于
笔墨书艺之间。

No intention on being an official

At the end of Eastern Han Dynasty, waiqi(relatives of a king or an emperor on the side of his mother or wife) and eunuchs were in power by turns, the society was very turbulent. Many kind and upright men fought back, such as Li Ying, Chen Pan, Wang Chang, etc., but they were either killed, banished, or poisoned. From then on, scholars were silent; people did not dare to speak. The whole country fell into disturbance and confusion. What's more, his father was framed up by powerful ministers and eunuchs, Zhang Zhi had no intention of pursuing an official career. So he declined all rewards from the emperor, and indulge himself in pen, ink, calligraphy and art.

二十九　携妻返乡

由于张芝无意仕途，对官场黑暗深恶痛绝，张芝准备带着妻子回乡。于是准备了两辆马车，一辆家人乘坐，一辆装载生活杂物和太尉陈藩赠予的几捆纸张及黄芙蓉带来的六匹白绸。一家人从京城出发，走过戈壁滩回到渊泉老家。

Take his wife home

Since Zhang Zhi had no intention in pursuing an official career and abhorred the darkness of the official circles, he prepared to take his wife home. So he prepared two horses, one for his family, the other for life sundries and a few bundles of paper sent by Taiwei(supreme government official in charge of military affairs) Chen Pan, as well as six plain silk fabrics brought by Huang Furong. The whole family started from capital, walked across Gobi desert, and came back to their hometown Yuanquan.

潜心书意

Focused on calligraphy

Zhang Zhi saw his father, who had made outstanding contribution to the country and was dedicated to the country and people, but was almost killed. So he abhorred the officialdom in which each tried to cheat and outwitted the other. He made up his mind to stay away from officialdom, and became focused and dedicated to the research of calligraphy art.

三十　潜心书意

张芝见沉浮宦海的父亲，虽功勋卓著，一心为国为民，也险遭杀身之祸，由此对尔虞我诈的官场深恶痛绝。他立志再不入仕途，潜心沉意研究书法艺术。

沙漠得宝
丙申年之夏云
董子于深圳

三十一 沙漠得宝

一日张芝惊闻有人在沙漠中发现了前朝竹简，他立刻赶往该地。在沙漠中驱驰数十里，来到了一座半塌的烽火台。张芝不顾一切地扑上前去，看到了散落在地上的几片竹简，再用手扒开浮沙，里面都是层层叠叠的竹简。张芝被这突如其来的收获感动得热泪盈眶。

Obtain treasure in the desert

One day, surprisedly, Zhang Zhi heard that someone found some bamboo slips of the previous dynasty in the desert, he immediately went there. He rode a horse for tens of miles in the desert and came before a half−collapsed beacon tower. Zhang Zhi went to the most extreme lengths to rush forward and saw a few bamboo slips scattered on the ground. He used his hand to push aside the sand, and find piles of bamboo slips. Zhang Zhi was touched to tears by this sudden harvest.

研读不惰

研读不惰。情丁酉年冬月書之振中空中 [印][印]

Study relentlessly

Zhang Zhi brought the bamboo slips back to Dunhuang. He immediately began to clear up those fragmentary bamboo slips. Some of the writing on the bamboo slips were honest, simple, elegant, and of classical beauty; some of them were like seal character (a style of Chinese calligraphy, often used on seals), some of them were like cursive hand (in Chinese calligraphy where characters executed swiftly and with strokes flowing together); they were graceful and natural. Zhang Zhi was overjoyed as if he had discovered a precious treasure. He was very excited. He buried his head in them and studied them all day, and didn't want to leave.

三十二　研读不惰

张芝带着竹简回到敦煌，他立刻开始整理那些残缺不全的竹简。竹简字迹有的敦厚朴实、端庄古雅；有的若篆若草、飘逸自然。张芝如获至宝，兴奋不已，整日埋头钻研，不肯离开一步。

不罢不休。

状如小山。他如痴如醉，墨磨万锭，

寝忘食，竹简写尽万片，置放堆砌，

毛笔磨秃千管，堆积成冢。他废

张芝练习书艺，孜孜不倦，

三十三　简山笔冢

Bamboo slips mountain
and writing brush tomb

Zhang Zhi was assiduous in practicing calligraphy. Thousand of his writing brushes were ground bold, forming a tomb. When he practiced, he disregarded meal times and go without sleep. He wrote on tens of thousands of bamboo slips. When they were piled up, they were like a small mountain. He was captivated in calligraphy and was entranced by it. He ground tens of thousands of inkstones incessantly.

圣柳思书 丁丑之夏月

Look at the willow and think about the calligraphy

Zhang Zhi learned from all famous teachers, but he always felt that his writing had many shortcomings. The feature of his writing couldn't be displayed. One day, when he was resting, he looked at the willows by the river. When he looked at the willows, the branches of the willow were intermingled with each other, they were swaying and hanging down, and they were very pretty and charming. Seeing this, he seemed to have realized something. He tried this feeling on his calligraphy. And it was very effective. The cursive hand (in Chinese calligraphy where characters executed swiftly and with strokes flowing together) was lively and graceful, he had made great progress.

三十四 望柳思书

张芝遍学名师，总觉书写技艺有颇多欠缺，书者个性，无法最大限度张扬。一日小憩，目光投向池畔之柳，盯着万千勾连、摇曳下垂之绿丝，在微风中婀娜多姿、千变万化，他似有所悟。他尝试将此感觉运诸笔端，果然有效，草书灵动飘逸，大有增进。

笔走剑势 丁酉年之夏月華振中

三十五　笔走剑势

时过不久，张芝习书后，总觉不尽人意，所写草书阴柔有余，阳刚不足，不禁长吁短叹。抬头见墙上宝剑长期不舞，已是尘土满鞘，不禁又想起当年随父沙场争战的情景，手中的剑不经意地舞了起来。只见剑如白蛇吐信，嘶嘶破风，又如游龙穿梭，行走四身，时而轻盈如燕，时而骤如闪电。舞着舞着张芝只觉此剑已变成一只毛笔，钩撇点捺皆合法度，挥洒自如，放荡不羁。张芝连忙放下宝剑，提笔习字，只见笔走剑势，譬如闪电，如龙似蛇，遒劲有力，至此张芝草书初步形成。

The writing of calligraphy is similar to swaying the sword

After a while and after Zhang Zhi practiced writing, he always felt unsatisfied. His cursive handwriting was full of feminine and tenderness and lacked masculinity. So he was unhappy and moaned and groaned. Looking up, he saw the sword which hadn't been practiced for a long time had been full of dust. He couldn't help but memorizing the days when he fight in the battles with his father. Then he began to practice the sword in his hand unconsciously. The sword was like a white snake disgorging its tongue, breaking through the wind; it was also like a dragon, shuttling and walking. Sometimes it's as light as a swallow, sometimes it was as fast as a lightening. Zhang Zhi swayed and swayed, then he felt that the sword had become a writing brush, the gou(hook stroke in Chinese characters, pie (left falling stroke in Chinese characters), dian (dot), na(right—falling stroke in Chinese characters), all conformed to the rules. The writing was free and wild. Zhang Zhi immediately put down the sword and took out a writing brush to practice. The writing brush resembled the sword and the thunder light, dragon and snake. The writing was powerful and strong. Until then, Zhang Zhi's cursive handwriting initially formed.

Jincao (a type of cursive
handwriting) initially formed

Zhang Zhi was not restricted by his predecessor's way of writing. He was brave and innovated. He jumped out of the
set pattern of Cui and Du, deleted dian (dot) and drew strokes, simplified what was complicated, created Jincao (a type
of cursive handwriting)and was unique in his style. Zhang Zhi's Jincao (a type of cursive handwriting) was accomplished
in one breath, the up and the down were linked together, the writing was continuous. Even when the writing was not
linked occasionally, the qi and channel were connected. Jincao (a type of cursive handwriting) was a symbol that Chinese
characters would no longer only have writing function, it made writing enter into a care-free and unconstrained free world.

三十六　今草初成

张芝没有被前人的笔法禁锢，
他勇于创新、跳出崔、杜的窠臼，
省删点画波磔，化繁为简，首创今
草，自成一家。张芝的今草一气
呵成，上下牵连，连绵不绝，偶
有不连，亦是气脉相通。今草第
一次将汉字从纯粹的书写功能中
剥离出来，进入了一个无拘无束、
汪洋恣意的自由境界。

评书论道

三十七 评书论道

书友聚会已成定例，这次笔会仇靖从山东曲阜带回两帖碑拓，一是《乙瑛碑》，再一为《礼器碑》，书法精湛，众人十分赞赏。再看每人所带新作，各有所长。当大家看到张芝新作，大吃一惊，人人称奇，无不为其所折服。张芝笑道：「草字可如画、如文、如舞、如歌、如诗。千种风韵万种风情，皆可由笔端流出。」

The book friend gathering had become a rule. In this pen gathering, Qiu Jing took two stele rubbings from Qufu, Shandong. One was *Yiying Stele*, the other was *Liqi Stele*. The calligraphy was exquisite and everyone liked them. Then they looked at the new works done by each person. They all have their advantages. When people saw Zhang Zhi's new work, they were astonished. Everyone wondered at it, they admired it. Zhang Zhi smiled and said, "cursive handwriting can be like painting, character, dance, song and poems. Thousands of charm and ten thousands of flirtatious expressions can be expressed by the writing brush."

Have an inspiration occasionally

One day, Zhang Zhi was practicing cursive handwriting. He was just excited about writing, but the bamboo slips for writing had been finished. The passion was still great in him, surging forward like a torrential tide. The momentum couldn't be stopped. Suddenly a thing came to his eyes: a plain silk aired in the yard. His heart leaped, he ran there and pull it down. His wrote on the plain silk with his writing brush which was like a snake and dragon. He was comfortable and carefree when he wrote. Then he finished the writing practice.

三十八　偶得灵感

一日，张芝练习草书，意兴正浓，竹简已用完。激情仍在心胸中涌动，汹涌澎湃，势不可挡。忽然院中一物跳入眼帘，乃晾晒之一条白绸。他心里一动，奔去扯下，于白绸之上，笔走龙蛇，酣畅淋漓，完成习作。

三十九　衣帛尽书

张芝练习书法，如醉如痴。凡达忘我之境。竹简、白绸写光，状态正佳，来不及去洗，就顺手取来自己衣服，当纸练字。家中其余衣帛也都被他写遍。晋卫恒《四体书势》曰："凡家中衣帛，必书而后练之。"

All silk and clothes were
written characters by him

When Zhang Zhi practice writing, he was completely entranced by writing, and almost forgot himself. All the bamboo slips and silk were written cursive handwriting by him, but he was on his best state. He didn't have time to wash, so he took his clothes to practice. Other clothes and silk at his home were also written characters by him. Jin Dynasty's Wei Heng wrote in his *Si Ti Shu Shi* (the earliest and a reliable book on calligraphy theory) that all clothes and silk in the house were written and practiced by him.

致良毛筆 丁酉年春王雪至陳州振中

Improve writing brush

When writing on silk, a lot of ink was needed. The dimension was great. The area of free writing expanded. The traditional writing brush moving between the small area of bamboo slip could no longer be used. Zhang Zhi was brave to improve it. He made the writing brush longer and larger, making the writing brush tip straight and firm and making it soft while tensile. The writing brush was then handy for writing. The calligraphers at that time all regarded it as a privilege to use the writing brush made by Zhang Zhi.

四十 改良毛笔

丝绸素帛吃墨多，尺幅大，自由挥洒扩大，原在竹简方寸之间移动的传统毛笔，难以胜任。张芝大胆改良，加长加大，使笔锋挺拔而健，柔中带韧，使用起来得心应手。当时书家，均以使用张芝制作之笔为荣。

四十一　一笔书成

张芝先将崔、杜笔法、烂熟于心，再吸取隶书并汉简之精髓，终于摆脱旧俗，独创一体，转精其妙，已成今草。字之体势，一笔所成，偶有不连，而血脉不断；字迹气脉贯通，隔行不断，其书如飞瀑惊电，若悬猿饮涧，又似钩锁连环，书成之时满纸风动，电闪雷鸣。古人谓之"一笔飞白"。从而开启了书法之二代新天地。

Write with one stroke

Zhang Zhi firstly memorized Cui and Du's writing methods proficiently, then absorb the advantage of Lishu(official script, an ancient style of calligraphy current in the Han Dynasty), and finally got rid of the old pattern and created a style of his own. He transferred the essence of his predecessors and created Jincao (a type of cursive handwriting). The structure, momentum and style of the writing were unique——they were written with one stroke. Occasionally the writing was not connected, but the channel was continuous. The writing's qi and channel were connected, when one line ended, and another line started, the writing was still continuous. His calligraphy was like a waterfall and thunder light, like a hanging ape drinking water, and like a hook and ring. When the writing was finished, the paper seemed to be moving with wind, and there seemed to be thunder light on his paper. The ancient people called it: one stroke caozhuan(a writing style of Chinese characters). A new era was started in calligraphy.

Not leaving out a cun of paper

Zhang Zhi created Dacao(a writing style of Chinese calligraphy)
and reached the climax of calligraphy art. Each work would make
people excited. At his time people treasured his works very much.
They compete to collect his works and didn't even leave out a cun
of paper. When he hadn't finished a work, there had already been
many people waiting and asking for his work. For a while his works
were very popular and his name was well-known in the nation.

四十二 寸纸不遗

张芝首创大草，达到书法艺
术巅峰。每幅作品都让人心潮澎
湃。时人极为钟爱珍视，争相收藏，
甚至寸纸不遗。一幅作品未完即
有多人等求。一时之间洛阳纸贵，
名动华夏。

四十三 力辞董卓

东汉末年，董卓入京把持朝政，挟天子以令诸侯，在"擢用天下名士以收众望"的大旗下，大规模提拔录用有名望的文人，蔡邕、许靖、韩馥等人皆受到重用。董卓亦数次征召张芝，张芝皆力辞，不为所动。

Decline Dong Zhuo

At the end of the Eastern Han Dynasty, Dong Zhuo entered the capital and arrogated power to himself. He controlled the emperor and commanded the nobles. Under the large flag of "Select famous scholars in the world to obtain fame and prestige", he selected and employed famous scholars. Cai Yong, Xu Jing, Han Fu, etc. were all assigned great tasks. Dong Zhuo also called up Zhang Zhi for many times, but Zhang Zhi declined and was not moved.

东行游学 丙申筆之秋月董振中

Travel eastward for study

In order to verify what he had learned, Zhang Zhi travelled eastward to study. When he went to a place, at that place, there would be an overwhelming cursive handwriting craze, very famous. The Jincao (a type of cursive handwriting) he created became popular very soon with great momentum. Meanwhile, when Zhang Zhi was free, he went to writing brush workshops to learn to make writing brush from the old craftsmen who made writing brush.

四十四 东行游学

张芝为验证所学，东向游学。所到之处，形成席卷一切的草书热潮，名噪一时。他所创今草，以不可阻挡之势，迅速风行大江南北。同时张芝在闲暇之际深入制笔作坊，认真向制笔的老艺人学习制笔工艺。

武威題銘
丁酉年之夏葉撰中

四十五 武威題銘

一篇銘文一蹴而就。

凝神題寫"澄華井"，并乘兴挥毫，

求张芝留下墨宝，张芝欣然提笔，

名澄华井。武威名士书家诚意恳

一井，水质甘甜，清冽沁凉，取

张芝东游武威，适逢武威新掘

Inscribe an epigraph in Wuwei

When Zhang Zhi was travelling east in Wuwei, there was a well newly dug in Wuwei. The water was sweet and cold. It was named Chenghua Well. The famous official and calligrapher in Wuwei earnestly begged Zhang Zhi to leave writing for them. Zhang Zhi wrote happily. He wrote "Chenghua Well", and wielded his writing brush while he was in high spirits. An epigraph was accomplished in an action.

___Receiving students___

Zhang Zhi received a lot of students. When he taught calligraphy, there were many students. A large number of famous noble scholars visited him for admiration of his reputation. They were from Luoyang, Chang'an, Tianshui, Dunhuang, Loulan and Gaochang. Liang Kongda and Jiang Mengying from Tianshui were famous noble scholars at that time, and their admiration for Zhang Zhi was even greater than Confucius and Yan Yuan.

四十六　开坛收徒

张芝广收学生，讲习书法，听者如云。从洛阳、长安到天水、敦煌，再到楼兰、高昌都有大批的名士慕名而来。天水梁孔达和姜孟颖都是当时名士，他们仰慕张芝甚至超过了孔子、颜渊。

尤不停歇。

破皮出血，指甲磨断，骨头外露，

手指头划地练字。以致手臂划伤，

时就手握草秆划墙，坐下来就用

弈游戏。他们效仿张芝令草，站立

然而他们相聚，不谈经论道，不博

张芝草书追随者俱是读书人。

四十七 皮破骨伤

All followers of Zhang Zhi were scholars. But when they gathered, they didn't talk about the classics or discuss the methods; they didn't play games. They imitated Zhang Zhi's Jincao (a type of cursive handwriting). When they stood, they held a straw to draw on the wall; when they sit down, they used their fingers to practice. In the end their fingers were hurt. The skin was damaged and there was blood. The fingernail was ground broken. The bone was exposed. But they still didn't stop.

Practice calligraphy in old age

At this time, Zhang Zhi had stepped into old age.
The cursive handwriting he created was grand.
All the viewers slapped the table and shouted with
praise. Although he had been famous in the whole
country, he still felt unsatisfied with his work. He
still practiced calligraphy everyday. He often had
new works which would surprise people.

四十八　暮年研书

此时，张芝已步入老年，所
创一笔草书，气贯长虹，炉火纯青，
观者无不拍案叫绝。虽然他已是誉
满华夏，然而每观自己所作，总有
不满之意。他仍然日日研书不辍，
总有新作不断问世，惊艳世人。

著书立说 丁酉年十一月 春子午

四十九　著书立说

张芝著有《笔心论》五篇，可惜早已失传。只在卫恒的《四体书势》中留下一句话：匆匆不暇草书。这句话让后世的书法家困惑了多年。钱钟书先生在名著《管锥编》中曾详细论证过『匆匆不暇草书』，他认为：此语乃张芝自道良工苦心也！

Write books and
establish theory

Zhang Zhi had written five pieces of Knowledge on Writing. But they were lost early. Only one sentence was left in Wei Heng's *Si Ti Shu Shi* (the earliest and reliable book on calligraphy theory): I am hurried; I am busy with practicing cursive handwriting. This sentence confused later generation calligraphers for many years. Qian Zhongshu used to carefully expound "I am hurried; I am busy with practicing cursive handwriting." in his famous work. He thought that this sentence expressed Zhang Zhi's feeling: to be a good calligrapher is a laborious work!

Recall with emotion before the diversiform−leaved poplar

In 191 A.D., Zhang Zhi had become an old man who was close to 70 years old. He was not as healthy as he used to be. He came before the 500−year −old diversiform−leaved poplar with the help of a crutch. He looked at the aged, strong and coiling diversiform−leaved poplar. The diversiform−leaved poplar's dragon−like body stuck out, standing upright perversely in the late wind. The leaves were golden, glittering under the setting sun. At this time, Zhang Zhi recalled the scene that he read and practiced calligraphy for thousands of times under the tree. He felt miraculous more as he looked at the tree more, completely forgetting himself. He seemed to experience a formless power, and felt deep respect for the tree involuntarily: ah! Diversiform−leaved poplar, you are indeed my teacher!

五十　胡杨感怀

公元一九一年，张芝已是年近
七旬的老人，身体大不如前。当
其手扶拐杖来到那棵已有五百年
树龄的胡杨树前，看着那苍老遒
劲的胡杨树，挺着蛟龙般的身躯，
在晚风中倔强地挺立着，片片树叶
在夕阳下，闪烁着点点金光。此时，
张芝回想起自己曾千百次在树下
看书习字的情景，不禁愈看愈奇，
如痴如醉，他似乎体味到一种无
形的力量，油然而生敬意……啊！
胡杨树，真我师矣！

五十一　魂归大漠

公元一九二年，张芝偶感风寒，卧床不起，数日不食。一冬日凌晨，白雪飘飘，天寒地冻，张芝含笑仙逝，驾鹤西去。东从洛阳，西至陇上，吊唁之人，络绎不绝。数百学子，哀声恸哭，其况空前。

His soul returned to the desert

In 192 A.D. Zhang Zhi caught a cold by chance. He stayed in bed for several days and didn't eat anything for quite a few days. On a winter day, early in the morning, there was the snow, the weather was cold and the ground was frozen. Zhang Zhi passed away with a smile. From the east to west, people offering condolence were in an endless stream. Hundreds of his students cried sadly. The scene was unprecedented.

五十二 五帖传世

东汉时期，人们珍视张芝墨宝已到了"寸纸不遗"的地步。尽管人们如此珍爱张芝墨宝，但张芝的书法作品存世极少。现在能看到的草书作品只有宋代的《淳化阁帖》中仅存的草书作品五幅，即芝白帖（又称秋凉平善帖）、知汝殊愁帖、今欲归帖和得郡阳帖，有人把知汝殊愁帖分为冠军帖和终年缠此帖。从冠军帖这件草书作品来看，它那宏大的气势、一往无前的气概，感人肺腑，堪称中国书法的千古绝品。

Five rubbing books were passed on

In the Eastern Han Dynasty, people treasured Zhang Zhi's calligraphy very much; they didn't even throw a cun of his writing away. Although people treasured Zhang Zhi's painting, few of Zhang Zhi's calligraphy were passed on to future generation. Now we can only see five cursive handwriting works in *Chunhua Pavilion Rubbing Books*, namely Zhibai, Qiuliangpingshan, I Know Your Worry, Today I Want to Return and Depoyang. Someone classified I Know Your Worry into Champion and Zhongnianchanci. The cursive handwriting work Champion had grand momentum and bold and powerful spirit. The work could move people deeply. This work could be named the unprecedented excellent work in China's calligraphy.

张芝书法对后世影响巨大，被

书法界誉为"万世师表"。晋草
书大家索靖乃张芝姊孙，善章草，
得张芝之法，时人称"靖得伯英
之肉"；书圣王羲之对张芝推崇
备至，师法多年，曾钦佩地说张
芝草书"好之绝伦，吾弗如也"；
狂草大师怀素自谓"草书得于二张"
（张芝、张旭）；唐朝草书大
家孙过庭亦把张芝草书当作蓝本，
终生临习，称"张芝草圣"，此乃
专精一体，以致绝伦。

五十三 万世师表

Zhang Zhi's calligraphy had an enormous impact on later generations. He was named "a teacher for ten thousands of generations" by the calligraphy circle. Jin's cursive handwriting master Suo Jing was Zhang Zhi's sister's grandson. He was good at Zhangcao (a specific kind of cursive handwriting of Chinese calligraphy). He obtained Zhang Zhi's calligraphy. The people of his time called it "Suo Jing obtained meat of Boying". Calligraphy prodigy Wang Xizhi accorded great importance to Zhang Zhi and learned his calligraphy for many years. He used to say with admiration that, "Zhang Zhi's calligraphy was matchless, I am not as good as him." Master of Kuangcao(an excessively free cursive style in Chinese calligraphy) Huai Su said, "My writing descends from Zhang Zhi and Zhang Xu." Cursive handwriting master of Tang Dynasty Sun Guoting also regarded Zhang Zhi's cursive writing as original version and practiced it all his life. He said, "Zhang Zhi's cursive writing is professional and proficient, that's way it is matchless."

大唐玄奘聖迹圖

DRAWINGS OF
XUANZANG SAINT
DEEDS IN THE
TANG DYNASTY

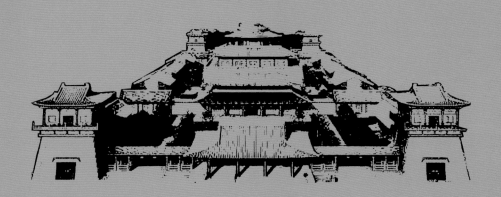

大唐玄奘

玄奘

Xuanzang

　　玄奘是举世闻名的佛学家、哲学家、旅行家、翻译家，中外文化交流的杰出使者，世界文化名人，是一个有理想有抱负的人。在他的身上体现着中华民族不屈不挠的"硬骨头"精神，真诚向外国学习的开拓精神，历尽千难万险、百折不挠的奋斗精神，不慕荣利、造福人民的爱国精神和国际主义精神，虚心不懈、寻求真理、攀登学术高峰的进取精神，融汇教内外各派理论的宽容精神，踏实、严谨的工作精神。玄奘的这些精神，正是我们应该发扬光大的。

　　玄奘是中国佛教史上的杰出高僧，中国文化的巨人，中国古代圣贤之一。他在中国乃至亚洲和世界文化史上具有不可替代的地位，他是中国精神的象征，是中国人永远的心灵导师，是中华民族的脊梁。

Xuanzang is a world famous Buddhist master, philosopher, traveller, translator, an outstanding envoy of the communication between China and the world and a world cultural celebrity. He is a person with ideal and ambition. From him, we can see the "hard bone" spirit typical of the Chinese people. He learns from the foreign countries earnestly; he has the following great spirits: the spirit of exploration, the spirit of fighting in the face of a multitude of difficulties and obstacles, the patriotism of not being after fame and fortune, the spirit of making contribution to people, the internaltional spirit, the spirit of being pious and unremitting, the spirit of searching for truth and climing the high mountains of academics, the recognition and torlerant spirit of integrating all theories of Buddhism and non-Buddhism and the rigid spirit of dependable work style. These spirits of Xuanzang should be promoted and developed by us.

Xuanzang is an outstanding and prominent monk of China's Buddhistic history; he is a giant of Chinese culture and one of the saints of China. He has irreplacable place in China, Asia and even world culture history; he is the symbol of Chinese spirit; he is the "soul tutor" of Chinese which will live forever; he is the back of Chinese people.

身出名门乙未年三春
宝圣深圳于年

一 身出名门

公元六〇二年，玄奘出生于河南偃师缑氏镇陈河村。姓陈，名祎。陈家是一个名门望族，他的祖父陈康，官至国子博士、国子司业和礼部侍郎。父亲曾任职江陵县令，其母乃洛阳长史宋钦之女。宋氏出身名门，贤达善良，懂诗书经典，笃信佛教，家族内皆敬重于她。玄奘从小受到父母良好的教育和熏陶。

Of noble birth

In 602 A.D., Xuanzang was born in Chenhe Village, Family Hou's County, Yanshi, Henan. His family name is Chen, and his given name is Yi. Family Chen is a notable family and great clan; his grandfather Chen Kang used to be the education officer of the highest educational administration and the vice minister of Ministry of Rites. His father used to be the county magistrate of Jiangling County, and his mother was the daughter of the head secretary of Luoyang Song Qin. Song was of noble origin; she was wise, able, understanding and kind; she could read poetry and the classics, and she believes in Buddhism, all members of the family respected her. Xuanzang received the good education and edification from his parents.

二 梦子远游

玄奘母亲怀孕期间，曾梦见自己的儿子英俊潇洒，身穿白衣，西去求法，母亲感到无比奇怪，就告诉了自己的丈夫，父亲也认为极其神奇，但也无法知道缘由。

梦子远游

甲午季大暑董振中

Dream of her son's travelling afar

During Xuanzang's mother's pregnancy, she used to dream that her son was handsome and unrestrained, wearing a white clothes and going to the west for Buddha dharma; her mother felt very peculiar, so she told her husband; his father also regarded it as extremely miraculous, but couldn't get to know the reason.

三 随兄出家

玄奘自幼聪慧，悟性甚高。他的启蒙老师是他的父亲，但是父母却分别在他五岁和十岁时去世，之后，他跟着在洛阳净土寺出家的二哥陈素（长捷法师）当了一名少年行者。

随兄出家

To become a monk with his brother

Xuanzang was very clever being a child and was extremely good at comprehension. His abecedarian was his father, but his parents died when he was five and ten years old. After that, he followed his second brother Chen Su (Master Changjie), who became a monk at Jingtu Temple, Luoyang, to become a teenager untonsured monk.

四 剃度受戒

公元六一二年，朝廷在洛阳度僧十三名，负责选拔僧才的隋朝大理寺卿郑善果得知陈祎有「远绍如来，近光遗法」的远大理想，就破格剃度，赐法名玄奘。二十一岁时，受具足戒。

Tonsured and being initiated into monkhood

In 612 A.D., the royal court tonsured 13 monks in Luoyang; the senior officer of Dali Temple of Sui dynasty, who was in charge of selecting monks, knew that Chen Yi had the great ambition of "in the long term, I wish to inherit the Buddha's dharma, and in the short term, I wish to promote and develop Buddhism", so he broke the rule and tonsured him, giving him the religious name of Xuanzang. By the age of 21, Xuanzang had already accepted bhiksuni.

五 发轫之初

剃度后的少年玄奘刻苦好学，十几岁时就在佛学上取得了显著的成就。

当时正值隋末唐初的动荡年代，但为了求得佛学真谛，玄奘下四川，上长安，辗转求学。出家十多年来，玄奘在国内遍访名师，质疑问难，精通了佛教的重要典籍，因而成为长安闻名的佛教界人物。他的学问愈广博，疑问也就愈多，为深究佛教真谛，萌发了到佛教发源地印度求法的强烈愿望。

The start of his religious path

After being tonsured, the teenager Xuanzang was assiduous and studious, and had achieved prominent accomplishments in Buddhism when he was still a teenager. At that time, it was the turbulent years of the end of Sui dynasty and the start of Tang dynasty, but in order to learn the true theories and essential ideas of Buddhism, he travelled to Sichuan and Chang'an for learning. During the years (over 10 years) of his monkhood, Xuanzang had visited all famous masters of Buddhism, asking others to solve difficult questions for him and repeatedly discussing and analyzing his doubts, so he became proficient in the important books of Buddhism and became a renowned figure in Buddhism circle of Chang'an. The more he learned about Buddhism, the more questions he had, in order to conduct in-depth research into the true theories and essential ideas of Buddhism, the idea of looking for Buddhism in India—the origin place of Buddhism, began to spring out of his mind.

六 矢志西行

玄奘二十五岁时辗转各地，向不同学派的大师求教，发现佛教各派理论不尽一致，许多问题都牵涉《瑜伽师地论》。他在长安遇见了印度僧人波颇，得知印度那烂陀寺的戒贤法师正在开讲《瑜伽师地论》，决定去印度求法。第二年，玄奘便联合几位志同道合的僧侣，向朝廷上表西行求法。因唐室新立，禁约百姓出蕃，被朝廷拒绝。然而玄奘却没有退缩。

Make up his mind to go to the west

At the age of 25, Xuanzang went to different places and learn from masters of different schools; he found that the theories of different schools of Buddhism were not completely the same, and many problems involved *Yogacara-Bhumi-Sastra*. He met Indian monk BoPo in Chang'an, and knew that master Shilabhadra was giving lectures on *Yogacara-Bhumi-Sastra*, so he made up his mind to go to India for his lectures. The next year, Xuanzang joined several monks with the same ambition and submitted a memorial to the throne. But since the Tang's dynasty was newly established, they prohibited ordinary people from exiting the country, so they were refused. But Xuanzang didn't withdraw from his ambition.

菩心磨砺 祈请加持
乙未年三春月於深圳董振中

七　菩心磨砺　祈请加持

他用人间种种艰难困苦试验自己，看自己是否经得起考验，于是玄奘几乎每天进入寺中，向菩萨启请，表明自己西行求法的心愿，请求菩萨加持自己一路顺利。

He used all sorts of difficulties and hardships in the world to test himself to see if he could endure the tests; he went into the temple everyday and expressed his wish of going west for Buddhism learning in the west, asking the Bodhisattva to protect and support his journey west.

八　冒越宪章　出关西行

贞观元年（627），天下大旱，灾情严重，玄奘法师随着逃荒的饥民，悄悄离开了长安，经秦州、兰州，到达凉州。

Broke the rule,cross the
pass and went west

At the first year of Zhenguan,
there was a great drought
around the nation, and the
situation of the disaster was
serious; Xuanzang, following
the famine victims who were
fleeing from the famine, left
Chang'an secretly, and arrived in
Liangzhou after passing Qinzhou
and Lanzhou.

凉州遇阻 甲午年孟冬之意 振中

九 凉州遭阻

当时唐朝的政权尚未完全巩固，西北一带边境时常受到西突厥的威胁，所以封锁边境，不准百姓私自出境。玄奘来到凉州遇到奉命守关的都督李大亮逼令还京。然而，玄奘受到慧威法师暗中帮助，偷渡出关，昼伏夜行到达瓜州。

Being stopped in Liangzhou

At that time Tang Dynasty's regime was not completely consolidated; the north-west border of the country was often threatened by Western Turkic Khaganate, so the border was locked and ordinary people were not allowed to cross the border without permission. When Xuanzang came to Liangzhou, he met the governor Li Daliang who observed the imperial order to guard the pass in Liangzhou; Li Daliang forced him to go back to Chang'an. However, Xuanzang was secretly helped by Huiwei Master and secretly crossed the border. He hid in the day and walked at night, and finally reached Guazhou.

十 滞留瓜州

瓜州刺史独孤达是一位虔诚的佛教徒，听说玄奘到来，非常欢喜，供养优厚，并劝说玄奘："西行路遥，必先渡葫芦河，后过玉门关，沿途有五座烽火台由官兵轮番把守，而大师孤身一人，且没有通关文牒，期间还有八百里流沙，您更是无法通过。"

滞留瓜州 乙未年春月 耀中

Being stranded in Guazhou

The prefectural governor of Guazhou Dugu Da was a pious follower of Buddhism; after hearing that Xuanzang came, he was very happy and joyful, and supplied Xuanzang with a lot of necessities of life; he persuaded Xuanzang that, the journey to the west was far and difficult; he had to cross Hulu River and pass Yumen Pass; during the journey there was five beacon towers which were guarded by the officers in turn. Xuanzang was all by himself; he had no document for passing the pass, and there was 800 miles of desert formed by flowing sands; it was even impossible to pass.

弘法阿育王寺乙未锋菱老衲

十一 弘法阿育王寺

玄奘听完，甚感忧虑，心想此去路途艰险，不妨在瓜州寺院里多待些时日，祈求诸佛菩萨加持护佑，于是就在瓜州的阿育王寺里讲经说法一个多月。在这期间，一路上陪他受苦受难的白马也因病死了，玄奘法师不禁悲伤万分。

Expounded the texts of Buddhism at Temple of King Asoka

After Xuanzang heard this, he felt rather worried; he thought that this journey was difficult and dangerous, he might better stay for some more time at temples of Guazhou to pray for the protection and support of various Buddhas and Bodhisattvas, so he expounded the texts of Buddhism at the Temple of King Asoka in Guazhou for over a month. During this period, the white horse which accompanied him and suffered together with him also died of a disease; Master Xuanzang was extremely sad.

十二　毁书劝行

瓜州州吏李昌也是个崇信佛法之士，他带着追捕的公文找到玄奘，问清原因后，深为玄奘西行求法的精神所感动，撕毁公文，请他及早西行，免得再生变故。

Destroyed the official
document and persuaded
Xuanzang to set off

Guazhou State Official Li Chang
was also a follower of Buddhism;
he found Xuanzang with the
official document of chase; after
asking clearly the reason, he was
deeply touched by Xuanzang's
spirit of pursuing Buddhism in
the west, so he tore the official
document apart and reminded
him to go to the west as early as
possible, in case any accidents
happened.

瓜州买马

甲午年夏董振中

十三　瓜州买马

李昌走后，玄奘越发愁闷了，慧威法师派来随行的两位小僧，道整已先去了敦煌，而留下来的慧琳身体单薄，又不堪长途跋涉，只好把他遣回凉州。自己虽买了一匹马，但苦于无人引路。

Bought another horse in Guazhou

After Li Chang left, Xuanzang became more depressed and dejected; the two young monks sent by Huiwei Master to follow him were useless—Dao Zheng had went to Dunhuang, and Hui Lin who stayed with him was not strong enough to endure the long and difficult journey, so he had to dispatch him to Liangzhou. Although he bought a horse already, nobody could help him and lead him the way.

十四 达磨之梦

有天晚上，瓜州东寺院里的一个名叫达磨的胡僧梦见玄奘坐在莲花上向西而去，达磨觉得奇怪，连忙向玄奘报告梦中之境。虽然此事被玄奘斥为虚妄，但心中却暗自欢喜，认为这是即将成行的好预兆，于是进入寺院道场，更加诚心祈求。

Dream of Damo

At one night, a foreign monk coming from the west at the East Temple of Guazhou named Damo dreamed that Xuanzang was sitting on a lotus and heading for the west; Damo felt very peculiar so he hurried to report his dream to Xuanzang. Although Xuanzang regarded this matter as delusive, he was happy inside; he thought that this was a good omen—his journey would be successful, so he went into the place for the rite to pray more sincerely.

十五　玄奘收徒

玄奘法师在瓜州城东的寺院里祈祷佛、菩萨给他赐一个向导，这时一个叫石磐陀的胡人来拜玄奘为师，并答应送他渡过胡芦河，通过玉门关和五烽。

Accept an apprentice

Master Xuanzang prayed for a guider at the temple at the east of Guazhou; at this time a northern barbarian tribe man named Shipantuo asked Xuanzang to be his master and he promised that he would help him cross the Hulu River, pass Yumen Pass and the five beacon towers.

十六　易马西行

第二天，石磐陀如约前来，并带着一位年老的胡人，牵着一匹又瘦又老的红马同来，石磐陀介绍："这位老人家对西行的路线很熟，来往伊吾三十多次，而这匹红马，不要看它既老又瘦，但它来回伊吾国，已经有十五次，不但脚力强健，而且能够识途。这样，玄奘听了石磐陀的话，便与老翁换马，毫不犹豫踏上了旅途。

Changed his horse and
went west

On the next day, Shipantuo came as agreed, and he brought an old Northern barbarian tribe man with him, holding an old and thin red horse; Shipantuo introduced, "this old man is very familiar with the path to the west; he has come to and fro Yiwu for over 30 times; this red horse, although it is old and thin, it has come to and fro Yiwu Country for 15 times; it can walk long distances and recognize the path." After listening to what Shipantuo said, Xuanzang changed his horse with the old man and started his journey west without hesitation.

板渡葫芦河 乙未年夏 董振中

十七 夜渡葫芦河

趁着夜色玄奘和石磐陀踏上了偷渡国境的道路，三更时分到葫芦河边，于是石磐陀斩木为桥，布草填沙，驱马前行，就这样玄奘师徒渡过了传说中水流湍急的葫芦河，玄奘又惊又喜，在遥远的天边已可以看到玉门关的影子。

Cross Hulu River at night

While it was dark, Xuanzang and Shipantuo started their journey of crossing the border secretly; at 00:00 they reached the Hulu River, so Shipantuo chopped wood and made a bridge, distributed the grass and filled in with sand, and drove the horse forward; in this manner Xuanzang and Shipantuo crossed the turbulent Hulu River; Xuanzang was surprised and overjoyed; he could already see the shadow of Yumen Pass in the distance.

十八　分道扬镳

玄奘法师与石磐陀一起驱马过河后，石磐陀想到家有妻儿老小，而他西行必被捉而杀之。他被前行的险途吓倒了，不愿意再前进。玄奘法师便放他回去，独自一人踏上了茫茫大漠。

Separate with Shipantuo

After crossing the river with Xuanzang Master, Shipantuo remembered that he still had wife and offsprings in the family; if he went west, he would definitely be captured and killed. He was scared of the dangerous journey ahead and was no longer willing to move forward. So Xuanzang Master let him go and walked onto the desert alone.

十九 王祥挽留

玄奘法师来到玉门关外见到了王祥校尉，王祥劝他不要冒险西行，可以前往敦煌去做法师，那里佛法兴盛，又有一位张皎法师，德学兼备，可以与他一起弘扬佛法。但玄奘不为所动，并发誓「宁可向西就死，绝不东归而生」。

Wang Xiang's detainment

Xuanzang came to the Yumen Pass and met Wang Xiang, the military officer; Wang Xiang persuaded him that he shouldn't risk his life to go to the west, and that he could go to Dunhuang and be a master there; the Buddhism was prevalent there, and there was a Zhang Jiao Master, who was possessed with high levels of morality and education; he could develop and expand Buddhism with him. But Xuanzang was not touched, and he swore that he prefered to die in the west rather than survive in the east.

二十　般若心经　禅定心诚

玄奘一个人走在无垠的沙漠里，四周所见，除了黄沙弥漫，见不到路的尽头。从白天到晚上，从黑夜到黎明，一路上，玄奘法师一直默念着观世音菩萨圣号及《般若波罗蜜多心经》，以排除内心恐惧。

Hannya Shingyo, focused on Buddhism, the heart was sincere

Xuanzang walked on the boundless desert; what he saw around was the permeating yellow sand, and he couldn't see the end of the road. From day to night and from night to dawn, Xuanzang Master had been reading the sacred title of Arya Avalokiteshvara and *Hannya Shingyo* to get rid of his fear.

二十一　绝域孤旅

莫贺延碛大沙漠是玄奘法师西行途中最艰难的里程。在沙漠中走了一百多里，遇沙暴迷路，找不到水源，下马取水时，又不慎将盛水的皮囊打翻，五天四夜没有滴水入口，终因体力不支昏倒在沙漠中。

A lonely journey at the impasse

Moheyanqi Desert was the most difficult part of Master Xuanzang's journey west. After walking for over 100 miles in the desert, Xuanzang encountered a storm and couldn't find the water source; when he jumped off the horse to obtain water, he overturned the water sac, and didn't drink anything for 5 days 4 nights; finally, he fell in the desert due to lack of stamina.

二十二　大漠惊魂

玄奘五天四夜滴水未进，口干舌燥，全身发烫，头晕目眩，连人带马栽倒在地上，奄奄一息，昏睡过去，梦见一个身高好几丈，傲然站立的巨人，威严叱喝他说："'为何不打起精神赶路，还躺在这里做什么？'"玄奘挣扎着站起来，继续前行。

A scary dream in the desert

Xuanzang didn't drink anything for 5 days and 4 nights; his mouth was parched and his tongue was scorched; he was hot all over; he felt dizzy and fell on the desert with his horse; he was at his last gasp and fell asleep; in his dream, there was a giant standing right before him and reproaching him solemnly, "stand up, go on your journey, why are you still lying here?" Xuanzang struggled and stood up, continuing his journey.

二十三 遇救野马泉

玄奘骑着大红马昏昏沉沉不知走了多久，大红马突然像发疯一样撒蹄狂奔，来到一处有青草和甘泉的地方，玄奘喜出望外，人马俱得重生。

Being saved at Wild Horse Spring

Riding his red horse, he was dizzy and sleepy; he didn't know how long he rode, his red horse suddenly began to run rapidly like crazy, coming to a place of green grass and clean water; Xuanzang was overwhelmed with joy; both he and his horse came back to life again.

二十四　伊吾遇故人

玄奘进入伊吾国境，来到一处寺院，寺院里的汉族僧人听说故乡的人来了，高兴得连鞋都忘了穿就跑出来迎接。一见面就抱着玄奘痛哭起来，哽咽了半天，说不出话来。

伊吾遇故人　甲午年笔夫宝坝中

大唐玄奘圣迹图

Met countrymen in Yiwu

Xuanzang entered the territory of Yiwu, he came to a temple; after the Han nationality monks heard that a monk from their hometown came, they all went to greet him, some of them even forgot to wear their shoes. When they saw Xuanzang, they cried loudly; they choked with sobs, couldn't say a word.

二十五　礼遇高昌国

高昌国王麹文泰崇信佛教，早闻玄奘法师大名，派使者盛邀玄奘到高昌国。玄奘不好推辞，走了六天六夜，翻过火焰山，到达高昌国（位于今吐鲁番）。高昌王下令大开城门，都城灯烛辉耀，王公大臣、宫女待从，簇拥着国王及王妃，分成两列，前后执烛迎接。

A polite welcome in the country Gaochang

The king of Gaochang Qu Wentai was a follower of Buddhism; he had heard about the great reputation of Xuanzang Master for a long time, so he sent an envoy to invite Xuanzang to Gaochang. Xuanzang couldn't turn him down, so he walked for 6 days and 6 nights, crossed the Mountain of Flames, and arrived at Gaochang (Turpan). The king of Gaochang ordered his soldiers to open the city gate; the capital city was lit by lights and candles; the princes, dukes, ministers and the imperial palace maids and servants clustered around the king and the queen, dividing into two lines and welcoming Xuanzang while holding candles.

二十六　宁可西行死　不可东归生

鞠文泰劝他留下共享荣华富贵，玄奘坚决拒绝。鞠文泰又以遣送他回国相威胁，玄奘表明：宁可西行而死，不可东归而生，遂绝食三日，以死明志。鞠文泰无奈，只好让玄奘为皇室成员讲了一个月的《仁王护国般若波罗蜜经》，两人又因相见恨晚而结拜为兄弟，并约定玄奘取经归来，再到高昌国讲经三个月。之后为玄奘准备了二十年往返的辎重和一队人马，亲自送他出境。

Prefer to die in the west rather than survive in the east

Qu Wentai persuaded him to stay and to live a life of great wealth and rank, but Xuanzang rejected him resolutely. Qu Wentai threatened him that if he didn't follow his will he would repatriate him to Chang'an, but Xuanzang indicated that he would die in the west rather than survive in the east, so he went on a hunger strike for 3 days, and demonstrated his determination with death. Qu Wentai was helpless, so he let Xuanzang taught Sutra for the royal family members for 1 month; the two regretted that they didn't meet sooner, so they became sworn brothers, and Xuanzang promised Qu Wentai that he would give lectures on sutra for 3 months after he finished his mission west. Later, Qu Wentai prepared materials for use of 20 years and a team of horses and servants, and sent him abroad in person.

寧可西行死　不可東歸生
甲午年之歲末　揽中

二十七　翻越大雪山

大雪山高峻险峭，冰雪聚积，终年不化，说话声音稍大，就会引起雪崩。玄奘一行吃住都在冰上，艰难跋涉了七天七夜，走出大雪山。同行人中，有三四成冻死在雪山上。走下大雪山，有一座高山湖泊，虽然周围被冰山所围，湖水却清澈见底，碧波荡漾，没有结冰，玄奘称它为"热海"。

Climb the great snow mountain

The great snow mountain was high, precipitous and risky; the snow and ice accumulated and wouldn't melt for the whole year; if one spoke slightly loudly, a snow slide would be caused. Xuanzang's team ate and lived over the ice; they trudged for 7 days and 7 nights and finally walked out of the great snow mountain. Among his travelling partners, 30%–40% of them died on the mountain. Walking down the great snow mountain, there was a high hill lake; although it was surrounded by the ice mountain, the lake water was transparent and the bottom could be seen; the surface of the lake rippled and there was no ice; Xuanzang called it the "hot sea".

二十八 可汗护法

又西行五百多里，玄奘来到碎叶城受到西突厥统叶护可汗的热烈欢迎和款待，走时可汗亲率群臣出都城相送十余里。玄奘西行数千里，越过险要关隘铁门关，进入今阿富汗境内的迦毕试国，看到一座沙落迦寺，此寺是汉代一位太子在这里做人质时修建的，寺内封存了许多珍宝，国王听说玄奘法师是从东土大唐来的，开启宝库，尽数供养。

Khan's protection

Xuanzang walked on west for another 500 miles and came to Suyab City where he was warmly welcomed and treated by Tongyehu Khan; when he left, he was sent off by his group of ministers for over 10 miles. Xuanzang went west for thousands of miles, passed the dangerous Iron Gate Pass, entered Jiabishi which was located in Afghanistan today; in Bijiashi, he saw a temple named Shaluojia; it was built by a prince of Han Dynasty, who was a hostage then; in the temple, a lot of treasure was locked; when the king heard that Master Xuanzang came from China of the east, he opened the treasury and use the treasure to support him.

二十九　参访佛国　礼拜圣迹

离开迦毕试国，由西北折向东南经今巴基斯坦，到印度境内。一路上玄奘遇到寺庙、佛塔就洒扫、参拜；遇到高僧大德就请他们讲授佛学理论，获益匪浅。他又走了一年，来到当年佛陀悟道的菩提树下，如同游子回家一样，百感交集，泪流满面，他五体投地，膜拜圣树。玄奘参拜圣树的活动整整进行了九天，实现了他参拜佛祖圣迹的愿望。

Visit the country of Buddhism and worship the sacred relic

After leaving Jiabishi, he turned to the southeast from the northwest and passed today's Pakistan and entered India. On the road, as long as Xuanzang saw a temple or pagoda, he would water it, clean it and worship it; as long as he met eminent monks or monks with high morality, he would ask them to teach him Buddhistic theories; this made him benefit a lot. He walked for another year, and came to the bodhi tree under which the Buddha realized the truth of Buddhism; when he came to the bodhi tree, he felt like a travelling son coming back home; all kinds of feelings welled up in his heart; his face was covered with tears; he threw himself down at the bodhi tree and worshiped it.Xuanzang's worship of the sacred tree lasted for 9 days; he realized his wish of worshipping the sacred relic of the Buddha.

三十　礼拜佛影窟

玄奘听说灯光城南二十余里处，有瞿波罗龙主所住的石窟，佛陀曾在此降服此龙，至今还留有佛陀的影像于窟内。玄奘法师前去瞻仰礼拜，途中遇到了五个强盗拔刀挡路，玄奘脱去帽子，现出庄严的僧像，不慌不忙地说：＂盗贼也是人啊，为了礼拜佛窟，毒蛇猛兽尚且不怕，何况你们都是人呢？＂强盗听了深感惭愧，竟发心随玄奘前往礼拜，玄奘执着地向石窟的东壁虔诚礼拜二百余拜，亲睹佛影出现后玄奘与众人深感惊奇，强盗们立刻毁弃了打劫用的刀杖，向玄奘求受五戒后离去。

Worship Foying Grotto

Xuanzang heard that 20 miles away from the south of Dengguang City, there was the grotto where Diboluo Dragon lived; the Buddha used to tame this dragon; until now, there was the shadow of the Buddha in the grotto. Master Xuanzang went there for worship and admiration; on his journey there he encountered five robbers who pulled out their knives and got in the way; Xuanzang took off his hat and revealed the solemn monk image, saying in a relaxed tone, "robbers are also human; in order to worship the Buddha Grotto, I am not afraid of snakes or beasts of prey, let alone humans." After hearing this, the robbers felt compunctious and even followed Xuanzang for worshipping; Xuanzang tenaciously and devoutly worshipped the east wall of the grotto for over 200 times; when he saw the appearance of the Buddha shadow, he felt extremely surprised, and so were the followers; the robbers immediately destroyed the knives and rods for robbing, and left after they received the five commandments from Xuanzang.

三十一　游学五印度

玄奘遍历印度，由北至中，由中至东，由东至南，最后至西印度，他不仅是中国周游印度的第一个旅行家，而且对于印度社会和佛教发展情况有了较为深刻的了解，因此，直到今天，印度的教科书里还记载着玄奘的事迹；在印度人民的心中，玄奘被称为『圣人』。

Travelled and studied
in India

Xuanzang travelled though the India, from the north to the middle, from the middle to the east, from the east to the south and lastly arrived at the west India; he was not only the first traveller to travel through the India in China, but also was the first Chinese who had relatively in−depth comprehension about Indian society and Buddhistic development in India, therefore, until now, India's textbooks still recorded Xuanzang's story; in India people's mind, Xuanzang was a saint.

三十二　遇难呈祥

玄奘法师一行人出了那罗僧诃城，向东行至波罗奢大森林，忽然遇到一群盗贼，有五十多人，把玄奘及随从的衣物全部夺走，并挥刀将众人押到一个干涸的池中，想要加以杀害，玄奘和一位沙弥机警地穿过草丛逃了出去，召集了一批耕田的婆罗门，有八十多人，大家拿着兵械冲进树林，强盗见状，四散逃跑了。

Being safe even in a disaster

Xuanzang Master and his servants walked out of Naluosenghe City, and went east to Boluoshe Forest; suddenly they met a group of robbers, whose number was over 50; they robbed Xuanzang and his servants' clothes away, escorted them to a dry pool and wanted to kill them; Xuanzang and an acolyte observantly crossed the thick growth of grass and fled; they convened a group of Brahman who were ploughing; there were over 80 people; all of them ran into the forest with weapons; when the robbers saw them, they fled scattering in all directions.

三十三 留学那烂陀

玄奘到印度时，摩揭陀国的那烂陀寺，已有几百年的历史了，经过历代的增修，规模宏大，它是印度最壮丽的佛教寺院和佛教的最高学府，也是印度的学术文化中心。这里有精通各类学术的学者，收藏了浩繁的大、小乘典籍，《吠陀经》以及天文、地理、医药、技艺等书籍。

Study in Nalantuo

When Xuanzang came to India, the Nalantuo Temple of Mojietuo had already had a history of several hundred years; after the rennovation and addition of different dynasties, its scale was huge; it was the most magnificent Buddhistic temple in India and the highest academy of Buddhism, and it was the academic and cultural center of India. Here, there were scholars proficient in all sorts of sciences and numerous Mahayana and Hinayana classics. And there were the Veda and books on astronomy, geology, medicine and artistry.

三十四 戒贤收徒

那烂陀寺住持戒贤法师已年过百岁，道行、学问为全国所景仰，大家尊称他为"正法藏"，他继承了大乘佛教弥勒、无著、世亲、护法诸大师的学说，对瑜伽、唯识、声明、因明等学理都有很精深的研究。玄奘拜戒贤为师，戒贤虽年事已高，但还是特意为玄奘开讲《瑜伽师地论》，历时十五个月。玄奘在此留住了整整五年，早晚不辍潜心学习，把这里全部的经、律、论通览了一遍。他博学的声名又一次盛传于印度。

Shilabhadra accepted an apprentice

The abbot of Nalantuo Temple Shilabhadra Master had been over 100 years old; his state reached in practising Buddhism and knowledge was admired and respected by the whole nation; people addressed him respectfully as "Zhengfazang"; he inherited the doctrines of masters of Mahayana such as Maitreya, Asanga, Vasubandhu and Dhammapala and he had profound and study of "Yoga", "Yoyacara", "Shengming", "Indian classical logic", etc.. Xuanzang formally acknowledged Shilabhadra as his master; although Shilabhadra had already been very aged, he still gave lectures on *Yogacara-Bhumi-Sastra* especially for Xuanzang for 15 months. Xuanzang stayed here for 5 years; he concentrated his attention on study day and night, and read all the Buddhistic classics, disciplines, and theory books. His fame of being erudite spread all over India again.

東漢張芝聖跡圖·大唐玄奘聖迹圖

绝处逢生慈航普度 甲午年孟夏容墨张中

DRAWINGS OF ZHANG ZHI SAINT DEEDS IN THE EASTERN HAN DYNASTY DRAWINGS OF XUANZANG SAINT DEEDS IN THE TANG DYNASTY

三十五　绝处逢生　慈航普度

玄奘法师与几十人乘船向阿耶穆佶国去朝拜圣迹，途中遭遇信奉突厥天神的强盗。强盗不但抢夺了全部财物，并且欲杀了玄奘作为神的祭品，此时玄奘深知自己难逃此劫，便澄心净意，一心专念弥勒菩萨，愿得往生内院，亲闻妙法，突然间，黑风四起，折树飞沙，浪涌船覆，贼人大惊，询问得知，玄奘是大唐来的高僧，立刻列跪忏悔，稽首饭依，愿弃刀枪，一心向善。

Being unexpectedly rescued from a desperate situation, the Buddha was fatherly and delivered Xuanzang from torment

Master Xuanzang, together with dozens of people, went to Ayemuji to worship the sacred relic; on their road there they encountered robbers who were followers of Tujue God; the robbers not only robbed them of all their property, but also wanted to kill Xuanzang as the sacrifice for god; Xuanzang knew that he could not escape from this disaster, so he cleared his mind and focused on reading Maitreya, wishing to be reborn in Sukhavati and listen to the Buddhist texts in person; suddenly, there were black wind, which broke off the trees and blew up sands, which gushed surf and overturned boats; the robbers were very surprised. After inquiry, they knew that Xuanzang was an eminent monk from China, so they knelt down in a row and confessed, kotowed and were converted to Buddhism; they were willing to abandon their knives and spears and be kind men again.

三十六　遍访名师

此后五年，玄奘先后师从如来密、师子忍和胜军等佛学名师，虚心请教，阅读了各国的藏书。后来满载而归，重回那烂陀寺，向戒贤汇报游学经历。

Learn from prominent masters

Five years from then on, Xuanzang learned from Buddhistic masters such as Rulaimi, Shiziren, Shengjun, etc.; he modestly asked for instructions from them, read the collected books of all countries and came back with fruitful results; then he returned to Nalantuo Temple and reported his study journey to Shilabhadra Master.

三十七　讲经那烂陀

贞观十四年（640），三十八岁的玄奘由戒贤指定他住持那烂陀寺全寺的讲席，玄奘博学多才的声名从此响彻印度。

Give lectures in Nalantuo

In the 14th year of Zhenguan (640 A.D.), Xuanzang, who was 38 years old, was appointed to host the Buddhism lectures of Nalantuo Temple; Xuanzang's great learning and great ability were spread over the India.

三十八　讲法曲女城　名震五印度

贞观十五年（641）正月，戒日王决定在曲女城召开印度的佛教学术辩论大会，主讲人就是玄奘。赴会的有十八国国王，熟悉佛教大小乘的僧侣三千余人。婆罗门和其他教派的教徒二千余人，那烂陀寺也派千余人赴会。与会的人大多是博学善辩之士，是印度学术界空前的大集会，印度各国聆听中国大师讲经说法者，先后多达五万余人，人头攒挤，象、舆、幢、幡、帐，遍布几十里。至今，印度人民还在津津乐道这次盛会。

Teach Buddhism
in Kanauj, become
renowed in India

In January of the 15th year of Zhenguan (641 A.D.), Jieri King decided to host an Academic Debate Convention of Buddism of India in Kanauj, and the keynote speaker was Xuanzang. Kings from 18 countries attended the convention; more than 3000 monks who were familiar with Mahayana and Hinayana attended the convention. More than 2000 followers of Brahmanism and other religious sects attended the convention, Nalantuo Temple also sent more than 1000 monks to attend the meeting. Monks who participated in the convention were mostly erudite and good at debating; it was an unprecedented convention of the academic community of India; there were more than 50000 people who listened to a Chinese master's Buddhistic lecture; it was very crowed at the scene; the cars, flags and tents were distributed for miles. Until now, Indian people were still taking delight in talking about this convention.

振中善之亲丁未年归心似箭

三十九 归心似箭

四十一岁的玄奘虽在国外游学十五载，但一直萦怀着遥远的祖国，当他求法的目的已经达到，就急于要返回大唐。曲女城大会闭幕后，他向戒日王表达了这一心愿。戒日王请他参加五年一度的无遮大会后再动身。当无遮大会结束，玄奘向戒日王辞行，戒日王和鸠摩罗王以及那烂陀寺的僧众等心中不舍，一再劝阻挽留，但都动摇不了他坚定的归国之心。玄奘动身之日，万人空巷，大家都来送行，依依惜别，满怀崇敬。

Anxious to return

Although Xuanzang, who had already been 41 years of age, had studied and travelled abroad for 15 years, he always had his homeland in mind; when his intention of learning Buddhism had been realized, he was anxious to return to China. After the closing of Kanauj convention, he expressed his wish to King Jieri; King Jieri invited him to attend the "Meeting Open to All" before he left. When the "Meeting Open to All" was closed, Xuanzang said goodbye to Jieri King; Jieri King and Jiumoluo King and the monks in Nalantuo Temple were reluctant to let him go, so they persuaded him to stay and detained him, but non of these could shake his determinant decision of returning to China. On the day of Xuanzang's return, the whole town turned to see him off; they were distressed at parting and was full of reverence.

四十　载誉归国

贞观十七年（643）春，玄奘取道今巴基斯坦北上，经阿富汗，翻越帕米尔高原，沿塔里木盆地南线，历时两年回到长安。玄奘此行，行程五万里，历时十七年。贞观十九年（645）正月二十五日，玄奘到达京城长安西郊，受到朝野僧俗的热烈欢迎。玄奘大师经过的城门被拥挤得水泄不通。从印度带回来的五百二十箧、六百五十七部佛经，成为中华瑰宝。

Come back to China with honor

In the spring of the 17th year of Zhenguan (643 A.D.), Xuanzang went north via Pakistan, Afghanistan, Pamirs and Tarim Basin and spent two years combing back to Chang'an. This journey of Xuanzang was 50000 miles long and 17 years long. On the 25th of January, 19th year of Zhenguan (645 A.D.), Xuanzang arrived at the west suburb of the capital Chang'an and was warmly received by governmental and non-governmental monks. The city gate passed by Master Xuanzang was full of people. The 520 clips and 657 volumes of Buddhistic classics become the treasure of China.

归国峰盛
况二天闻
久天闻
名甲午
年之
大雪
拄深
圳董
振中

四十一 归国成盛况 天下久闻名

贞观十九年（645）正月二十五日，四十三岁的玄奘法师在离开祖国十七年、行程五万多里，历经一百三十余国后回到京城长安。这时，唐太宗正在东都洛阳，委托左仆射梁国公房玄龄、右武侯大将军侯莫陈实等出城迎接。次日举行了隆重的欢迎仪式，朱雀大街上人山人海，幡乐在前，僧侣在后，百姓载歌载舞，男女信众烧香散花，争睹玄奘法师风采。

Become a grand phenomenon in China, be celebrated for a long time

On the 25th of January, the 19th year of Zhenguan (645 A.D.), Xuanzang, who had been 43 years old, after left China for 17 years, after walked for 50000 miles, after passing more than 130 countries, returned to Chang'an. At that time, Emperor Taizong of Tang was at the east capital Luoyang; he entrusted the left prime minister and the State Duke of Liang Fang Xuanling, Wuhou General Hou Mo, Chen Shi, etc.to welcome Xuanzang outside the city. The next day, a grand welcoming ceremony was held; on the Zhuque Street, people were crowded, the Fan music (the sacrifice music played at Buddhistic ceremony) was played at the front, the monks were at the back; the common people were singing and dancing and the male and female followers were burning joss sticks and scattering flowers; they rushed to see the mien of Xuanzang Master.

四十二 呕心沥血 殚心译经

同年三月一日，玄奘奉诏到长安弘福寺，开始了他大规模翻译佛教经典的准备工作。

从五月开始，玄奘埋头译经，直到他逝世前的一个月，勤奋不懈地努力了十九年。在他的主持下，一共译出佛教的经，论七十五部，一千三百三十五卷，一千三百多万字。他是中国历史上译经最多的法师、新译的创始者、中国翻译史上最杰出的代表，为中国文化源资源宝库留下了最为珍贵的财富。

Exert his utmost effort, rack his brains to translate the Buddhistic classics

On March 1st of the same year, Xuanzang received the emperor's order to prepare for translating Buddhistic classics at Chang'an Hongfu Temple. The preparatory work was of large scale. From May, Xuanzang buried his head in translating; he had translated assiduously for 19 years and hadn't stop until his death. Under his hosting, 75 Buddhistic classics and lun, 1335 volumes and 13 million words were translated. He was the master that translated the largest number of Buddhistic classics, the founder of new translation and the most outstanding master in China's translation history, leaving the most precious treasure for China's cultural resource treasury.

四十三 觐见太宗

不久，太宗在洛阳积翠宫仪銮殿接见了玄奘，并给予了很高的礼遇。太宗敕令玄奘将印度见闻编写成书。太宗见玄奘气宇轩昂，见多识广，是一位可辅佐国家的栋梁之才，就劝他还俗辅政。玄奘婉言相谢，表示自己只想把带回来的佛经翻译出来。太宗命房玄龄负责译经事宜，一切费用由国库提供。

Have an audience with Emperor Taizong of Tang

Not until long, Emperor Taizong of Tang met Xuanzang at Imperial Regalia Hall of Jicui Palace, Luoyang, and treated him with great honor. Emperor Taizong of Tang ordered Xuanzang to write what he saw in India into a book. Xuanzang had a dignified appearance; when Emperor Taizong of Tang saw him, he regarded him as a man of tremendous promise that could help with the governance of country, so he persuaded him to resume secular life and assist with the governance of his country. But Xuanzang refused in gentle words, saying that he only wanted to translate the Buddhistic classics he brought home into Chinese. So Emperor Taizong of Tang ordered Fang Xuanling to be in charge of the translation of Buddhistic classics and all expenditure shall be borne by the state treasury.

四十四　殚心译佛经　尽瘁报国恩

玄奘回到长安，立即召集大德高僧二十多人到大慈恩寺，组建了一个庞大的国立译经场，开始翻译佛经，同时用一年的时间口述完成《大唐西域记》著述。贞观二十二年（648），四十六岁的玄奘翻译完《瑜伽师地论》后，应召去铜川玉华宫向太宗介绍了该经的大意，太宗亲览经卷，甚为欢喜，下令抄写九部，分发国内九州。

Rack his brains to translate the Buddhistic classics and spare no effort to return the favor of the country

After Xuanzang returned to Chang'an, he immediately convened more than 20 senior monks to Dacien Temple and established an enormous state translation place and began to translate Buddhistic classics; meanwhile, he spent one year in writing the book *Travelling Notes of the Western Regions in Great Tang Dynasty*. In the 22nd year of Zhenguan, After Xuanzang (46 years old then) had translated *Yogacara-Bhumi-Sastra*, he introduced the general idea of this book to Emperor Taizong of Tang in Yuhua Palace, Tongchuan; Emperor Taizong of Tang read the Buddhistic texts in person and liked it very much, so he ordered his cultural officials to write 9 copies and deliver them to the 9 states of the country.

大唐玄奘圣迹图

DRAWINGS OF XUANZANG SAINT DEEDS IN THE TANG DYNASTY

四十五　太宗作序

玄奘请唐太宗为他翻译的佛经作序。八月四日，太宗写下了著名的《大唐三藏圣教序》。序文中，太宗称赞玄奘为「法门之领袖」。太子李治也写了一篇《述圣记》的序文。这两篇序文都刻于碑石，立在西安大慈恩寺大雁塔下。

Emperor Taizong of Tang wrote the preface for him

Xuanzang asked Emperor Taizong of Tang to wrote prefaces for the Buddhistic texts he translated. On August 4th, Emperor Taizong of Tang wrote the famous *Preface for the Sacred Texts of Tang Sanzang*. In the preface, Emperor Taizong of Tang acclaimed Xuanzang as "the leader of Buddhistic study". The prince Li Zhi also wrote a preface named *A Story of the Sacred*. Both of them were carved on stones and were established before the Greater Wild Goose Pagoda of Xi'an Daci'en Temple.

四十六 入住西明寺

显庆三年（658）正月，玄奘随高宗自洛阳返回长安，奉旨入住新建的西明寺译经。然而，在从印度归来后十多年的译经生涯中，玄奘很愧惜唐以前译出的一大部《大般若经》残缺多讹，玄奘遂决心重译，并想从瑜伽学上通于般若。但此经卷帙浩繁，而"京师人众，竞来礼谒"，庶务杂沓，无法静译。

In the January of the 3rd year of Xianqing (658 A.D.), Xuanzang followed Emperor Gaozong of Tang to return from Luoyang to Chang'an and followed his order to translate Buddhistic texts at the newly-built Ximing Temple. Xuanzang had been translating Buddhistic texts for over 10 years, but he regretted that the Mahaprajnaparamita Sutra which was translated before was not complete and had a lot of mistakes, so he decided to translate it again. But this Buddhistic book was of great length, and "there were a lot of people in Chang'an; they all came to pay tribute to him"; he was often disturbed by all sorts of business and could not settle to translate.

四十七　万法为寺

玄奘遂忆起十年前太宗召他去避暑的玉华山，那里近京僻静，山绿水清，鸟语花香，是个非常理想的译经场所。便向高宗呈上《重请入山表》，得到允准。玉华寺佛经译场，是玄奘一生中最重要的道场，是他一生译经最多的地方，是一所特具殊荣的中华译经圣地。

A new temple

Xuanzang then remembered the Yuhua Mountain where Emperor Taizong of Tang summoned him to get away from the heat ten years ago; that place was close to Chang'an and quiet; it had green mountains and clean water and was full of birds' twitter and frangrance of flowers; it was an ideal place for translating Buddhistic texts. So he submitted *Memorial- To Enter into Yuhua Mountain Again* to Emperor Gaozong of Tang and was permitted. The Yuhua Temple Translation Place was the most important Buddhistic place in Xuanzang's life; it was the place where he translated the most of his Buddhistic texts; it was a sacred place of Buddhistic texts translation with special honor.

四十八　大般若经　人天至宝

公元六六三年十月二十三日，玄奘带领弟子翻译六百卷的《大般若经》，他对译场的弟子们说：「玄奘今年六十有一，必当猝命于此迦蓝，经部甚大，每惧不终，人人努力加勤，勿辞劳苦。」历经三年，玄奘带领众弟子，终将六百卷《大般若经》圆满完成，成为镇国大典，人天至宝。

Mahaprajnaparamita Sutra, a treasure on earth and in heaven

On October 23rd, 663 A.D., Xuanzang led his students to translate the *Mahaprajnaparamita Sutra* which included 600 volumes; he said to his students at the translation place, "I have been 61 years old, I will definitely die at this temple; this Buddhistic book is huge, and I worry that the translation cannot be finished, so please work hard and diligently, and do not shirk your responsibility." After 3 years, Xuanzang finally finished the translation of *Mahaprajnaparamita Sutra* with his students; the Buddhistic book became a country guarding classic and a treasure on earth and in heaven.

四十九　预知时至　吩嘱后事

玄奘译完《大般若经》后，觉得自己身体大不如前，已预知无常将至，剩下的时日已经不多，就向弟子交代后事说："若无常后，汝等遣我宜从俭省，可以蓬蒉裹送，仍择山涧，勿近宫寺。不净之身，宜须屏远。"众弟子听后无不流泪。

Aware of his time,
instruct and entrust
his funeral affairs

After finishing the translation of *Mahaprajnaparamita Sutra*, Xuanzang felt that his health state was not as good as before, so he knew that his would die soon and didn't have much time left, so he instructed his students about his funeral affairs, "After I die, you should bury me in a simple manner; you can cover me with a rough bamboo mat, and put me among the mountains and away from palaces and temples. My body is not clean; it should be thrown to a place far away." All of his students cried after hearing this.

五十　法師圓寂　千古一僧

唐高宗麟德元年（664）正月初九傍晚，玄奘法師在肃成殿房后渡渠时不慎摔了一跤，虽然只是一点皮外伤，却病势沉重，昏迷不醒。直至正月十六日才如大梦初醒说："吾眼前有白莲花，大于盘，鲜净可爱。"二月初四半夜，玄奘的呼吸逐渐微弱，不久就圆寂了。送葬的这天，长安城及诸州五百里内的僧尼道俗，赶来送葬的有一百多万人。

The master passed away, becoming a saint of a thousand years

At the dusk of January 9th, the first year of Linde, Emperor Gaozong of Tang (664 A.D.), when Master Xuanzang was reading Buddhistic texts at Xiaocheng Palace, he fell down accidently; although it was only skin trauma, the state of the illness was serious; Xuanzang was in a coma. He didn't wake up until the 16th of January; when he woke up, he said, "I dreamed that there was a white lotus before me, which was larger than a plate, and was clean, fresh and lovely." In the midnight of February 4th, Xuanzang's breath gradually became weak, and passed away soon. At the day of funeral procession, monks and nuns from Chang'an and surrounding states all participated in the funeral procession; together there were more than 1 million people who came to see him off.